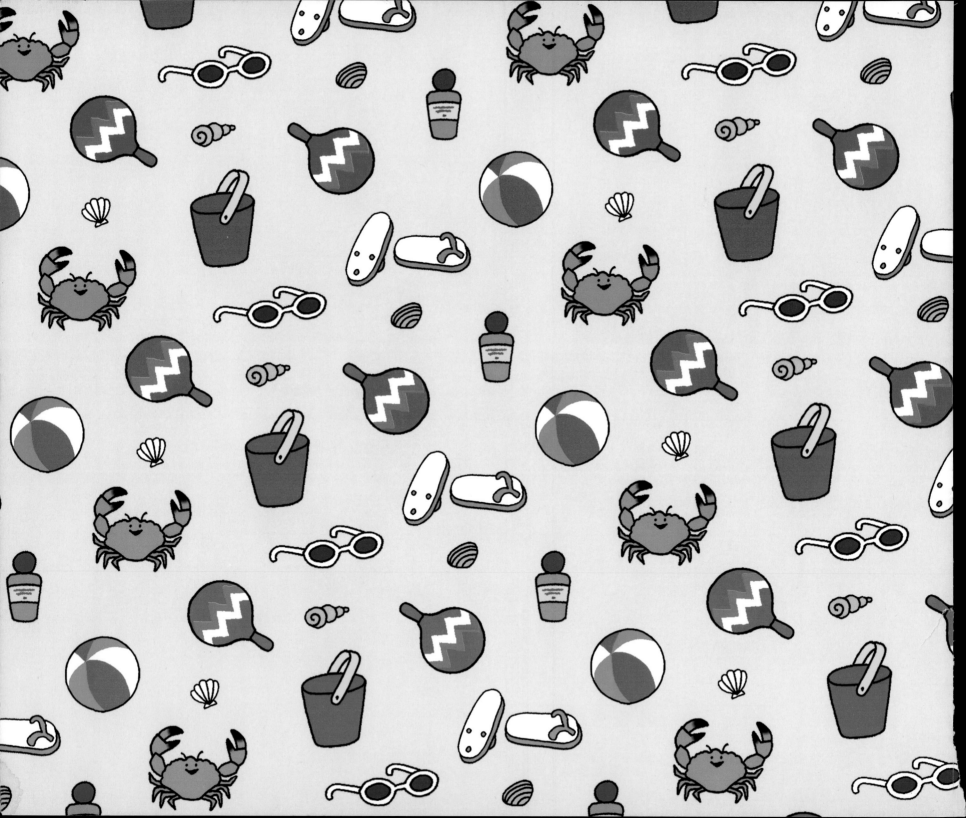

For Martha – J.D.
For Marco – N.S.

First published 2009 by Macmillan Children's Books
This edition published 2010 by Macmillan Children's Books
a division of Macmillan Publishers Limited
20 New Wharf Road, London N1 9RR
Basingstoke and Oxford
Associated companies throughout the world
www.panmacmillan.com

ISBN: 978-0-230-70648-4

Text copyright © Julia Donaldson 2009
Illustrations copyright © Nick Sharratt 2009

5 7 9 8 6

A CIP catalogue record for this book is available from the British Library.

Printed in China

Toddle Waddle

Written by
Julia Donaldson

Illustrated by
Nick Sharratt

MACMILLAN CHILDREN'S BOOKS

Toddle

waddle.

Flip flop,

toddle waddle.

toddle waddle.

flip flop, toddle waddle.

Ting-a-ling, clip clop,

hurry scurry, flip flop, toddle waddle.

Leap creep, ting-a-ling, clip clop,

toddle waddle.

hurry scurry,

flip flop,

Stop!

Boing boing, splish splash, puff puff,
roly-poly, crunch munch, slurp slurp,

chitter chatter, helter-skelter,
see-saw, snip snap, ping pong.

Flitter flutter,
buzz buzz,
leap creep, ting-a-ling, clip clop,

hurry scurry, flip flop, toddle waddle.

Bye-bye!